READ with me!

Let's play

by WILLIAM MURRAY
stories by JILL CORBY
illustrated by CHRIS RUSSELL

Ladybird Books

Tom

READ with me! *has been written using about 800 words and these include the 300 Key Words.*

In the first six books, all words introduced occur again in the following book to provide vital repetition in the early stages. The number of new words increases as the child gains confidence and progresses through the stories.

After Book 6, a wider range of vocabulary is used but each word is repeated at least three times within that story.

The stories centre on the everyday lives of Kate, Tom, Sam the dog, Mum, Dad, friends, neighbours and relations. This setting often provides a springboard into Tom and Kate's world of make-believe. Also, the humorous, colourful illustrations include picture story sequences to stimulate the reader's own language and imagination.

A complete list of stories is given on the back cover and suggestions for using each book are made on the back pages.

Further details about this reading scheme plus a card listing the 300 Key Words are contained in the Parent/ Teacher Guide.

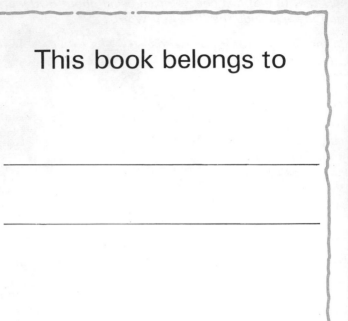

This book belongs to

_____

_____

British Library Cataloguing in Publication Data
Murray, W. (William), *(date)*
 Let's play.
 1. English language—Readers
 I. Title   II. Corby, Jill   III. Russell, Chris   IV. Series
 428.6
 ISBN 0-7214-1314-5

First edition

Published by Ladybird Books Ltd Loughborough Leicestershire UK
Ladybird Books Inc Auburn Maine 04210 USA

Printed in England

Kate

Here is Kate.

Here is Tom.

Here is Sam.

Sam is a dog.

Here is Kate and
here is Sam.

No, no.

Tom is in here

and Sam is in here.

Kate likes the dog
and Tom likes the dog.

Sam likes Tom and
Sam likes Kate.

No, Sam, no.

I like Tom.
I like Kate.

I like the dog.

Here is Tom

and here is Kate.

No, Sam, no.

Here is a shop.

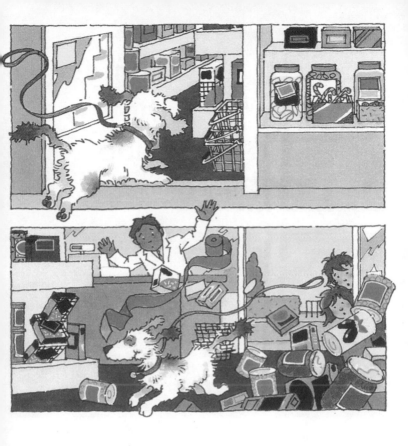

The dog is in
the shop.

Tom is in the toy shop.

Kate is in the toy shop.

Sam is in
the toy
shop.

Sam has a toy.
Sam likes the toy.
No, Sam, no.

Kate and Tom
like the ball.

Sam likes the ball.

The dog has the ball.

The dog likes the ball.

Here is a tree.

The ball is in the tree
and Tom is in the tree.

Tom has the ball.

Tom and Kate
like the ball.

Sam has the ball.

No,
Sam,
no.

Sam has no toy.

Sam has the toy.
Sam likes the toy.

I like Kate and
I like Tom and
I like Sam.

Words introduced in this book

Pages	
4/5	Tom, Kate
6/7	Here, is
8/9	Sam, a, dog
10/11	and, here,* no,* No
12/13	in
14/15	the, likes
18/19	I, like
22/23	shop
24/25	toy
26/27	has
28/29	ball
32/33	tree

Number of **different** words used. 18

* The same word, with and without a capital letter is shown as it appears in the book.

All are Key Words, with the exception of the three names, ie Tom, Kate, Sam.

These 18 words are all carried forward into the following book, Book 2 *The dragon den*.

Read these words.
Which word goes with each picture?

Tom   Kate   Sam   ball

Notes for using this book

The words, pictures and planning of this book are designed to:

* help the child to learn to read
* help you to make learning an exciting and enjoyable experience for her*
* encourage lots of conversation
* help her to become confident in her own ability
* encourage her powers of observation, understanding and sense of humour.

When your child is ready and keen to learn to read (a Reading Readiness checklist is given in the Parent/Teacher Guide) introduce this book just like any other picture storybook. Find a quiet, comfortable place and either read the book all the way through or read and talk about one page at a time. Point to the words and show that reading goes from left to right.

To avoid the clumsy he/she, him/her, we have referred to the child as "she". All the books are of course equally suited to both boys and girls.